Remembering the Magick

Fairy Tales for Those Lost, Found, or Wandering

Shirl Knobloch

• • •

Remembering the Magick: Fairy Tales for Those Lost, Found,

or Wandering

Edited by: Jennifer Sabatelli

Cover/Photography by: Shirl Knobloch

ISBN 13: 978-0-9974752-9-6

• • •

Also By Shirl Knobloch:

Birdsong, Barks, and Banter: Adventures of an Animal Intuitive Reiki Master and Her Home of Misfit Companions

The Returning Ones: A Medium's Memoirs

You're Never Too Old for Fairy Tales

Reenactments from My Heart: Spiritual and Supernatural Civil War Fiction and Poetry

Once Upon a Fairy Tale

Strength of a Lion, Soul of a Lamb: A Collection of Wolfhound Fairy Tales and Poetry

My Ten Legged Journey: The Road to Rainbow Bridge

Waiting for the Next Village Attack: Growing Up Italian, a Jersey Girl Reminisces

Enchanted: Fairy Tales for Young and Old

The Voice of Their Hearts: Learning Animal Communication

• • •

"Obsessed by a fairy tale, we spend our lives searching for a magic door and a lost kingdom of peace."

—*Eugene O'Neill*

• • •

...

Table of Contents

• • •

• • •

The Cobbler and His Mice

Once upon a time, in a river village of thatched cottages and heathered moors, there lived a cobbler. He had no children, and his wife had long passed. He spent his hours at his workbench, cobbling away at the village peoples' shoes.

Money was scarce. Most paid his fee in vegetables or farm eggs, but that was fine with the old cobbler. His needs were few.

The cobbler lived by himself, but his house was full. For you see, he loved mice. Others shooed them away (excuse the pun), but not the cobbler. His workshop shoes often served as beds for little mice when the hearth fire burned low and the cobbler lay fast asleep.

Scraps of leather served the mice well; they stitched together tiny coats. Scraps and crumbs of food that fell to the floor as the cobbler hammered at new soles fed them each day. The cobbler wasn't much for sweeping, so crumbs were always plentiful and little mice bellies grew full and strong.

Then, one autumn, a terrible plague came to the village. People blamed the cobbler and his mice. "Disgusting rodents," they whispered in the country lanes. "Disease-spreading vermin," they shouted as they passed his doorway, holding handkerchiefs up to their mouths. People started dying, and villagers became angrier and angrier with the gentle man and the innocent friends who never ventured from his walls.

One night, someone tossed a burning log onto his roof. The thatch caught fire quickly. The cobbler was asleep. Instantly, scores of little mice tugged at his blankets, tugged at his beard, and shrieked for him to awaken.

He woke to smoke filling his cottage and workshop. He raced in to save his cobbler tools, but he put them down when he saw *them*. So many baby mice huddled in his shoes with their frightened mamas' eyes piercing through the darkness. The cobbler picked up his toolbox, turned it upside down, and tossed out all his tools. Quickly, he picked up each shoe filled with tiny babies and their moms and placed them inside his toolbox, running out to the safety of the deep woods. The other frightened mice all scurried behind him.

It was a cold autumn night. The cobbler watched the light in the sky and knew his home was burning. What would he do? He had no cobbler tools, he had no home, and no one in the village wanted to be near him. With a heavy heart, he fell asleep, covered in fallen autumn leaves.

Little did he know that mice have friends, hundreds and hundreds of friends in the forest. All night long, tiny mouths formed mud from the river and carried sticks and branches to a clearing nearby. They built walls tall enough for a man. They carried pieces of thatch in their mouths and scaled the high walls to make a cozy roof. More and more came by the hour, and by daylight, their tiny cottage was finished.

When the cobbler opened his eyes, he could not believe what he saw. He spied a perfect little cottage, his toolbox placed at the doorway. He walked inside and found all the tiny shoes placed by a hearth, filled with happy children and their mamas.

He saw a stash of seeds carried inside that would give him spring crops when planted. A tall pile of kindling sticks laid waiting for a warm hearth fire. He would get by—no, *they* would get by. His tiny friends would see to that. For in the corner, there was one tiny cobbler's hammer. How they managed to carry it out mystified the man, but he smiled in gratitude.

The Fairy Queen's Crown

Once upon a time, in a forest of ancient trees and standing stones, there lived a Fairy Queen. Most beautiful she was, adorned in jewels and silver threads of spider silk.

One extremely windy day, a terrible accident happened. A gust of Irish wind blew her jeweled crown high into the sky! Away, higher and higher, it moved; soon, no glimpse of its sparkle shone in the sky.

"Oh no!" the heartbroken queen cried. "What shall I do without my crown?"

The Fairy Queen was dearly loved. News of her loss spread throughout the land. Her sobs were carried by the same Irish wind, telling all of her sorrow. The foxes hunted, the squirrels searched, and the birds cast their eyes to all the crevices of cairns, but her crown could not be found.

A fairy meeting was held. All the elves and woodland animals were invited. "What can we do?" they cried. "We have no jewels, no wires of gold and silver. How can we make a crown worthy of our beautiful queen?"

Nevertheless, their love was so great for their lovely Queen that work began instantly among the fairies and their friends. Branches were collected by the hedgehogs and foxes.

Berries were carried by the squirrels and mice. Fairy children collected leaves and moss from the forest floor.

Wisteria vines were twisted and woven into a crown to fit her head. Dried berries and leaves were entwined among the branches. Shimmering sea glass from the Irish coast was carried in by woodland birds. Chips of sparkling mica were gnawed and broken by the teeth of little mice and squirrels, and spider silk was threaded around it to hold it in place. The crown sparkled and shone like jewels.

"It isn't good enough!" moaned the fairies. "We have no diamonds and rubies, and there are no emeralds or sapphires! All we have is some glass and chips of rock!"

Little did they know that the Fairy Queen had been watching. Suddenly, she spoke, "It's the most beautiful crown I have ever seen!"

With that, she walked to the center of the fairy ring, picked up her crown, and delicately placed it on her head. She took two thistle thorns from the pocket of her gown and secured it to her hair. "Now, the wind will never carry it away again. Thank you so much, my friends. You have given me the most beautiful crown, worthy of a Fairy Queen!"

The fairies danced and the woodland creatures chirped and squeaked with delight. The Fairy Queen's crown sparkled in the sun, just like the smile that shone across her beautiful face.

"Do you really like it?" the animals and fairies asked. "It isn't real anymore."

"Why, isn't real?" the queen answered. "This crown is more real than any diamonds and gems. It is made out of all that I love, made by all whom I love. I wouldn't change it for all the jewels of a kingdom."

~~~~~~~~~~~

Meanwhile, halfway across the Isle, a mother and father sat helpless at their infant daughter's crib. "What shall we do?" the mother sobbed. "We've no food, no money for medicine, and her fever grows worse."

A weary father rose to go and work his dry field. "Dress warm," his wife said. "There's a bristling wind out there. I cannot care for the two of you sick in bed."

Little did they know that stuck in the briars was the answer to their prayers.

Somewhere in Between

All my life I have felt

Somewhere in between

Two sides of a coin

The kindness and mean

Between fairy tales, fate,

And fairies of lore

Between bullies of hate

And energy's door

Between realms of the living

And voices of the dead

All my life has been

Joined

By two sides in my head

From the place I was born

To a land where I dreamed

Far across a large pond

Where all friends dwelled

It seemed

Perhaps that is why

My heart yearns for the sea

And the place of belonging

It offers for me

Nowhere on this earth

Do I feel as serene

As that ocean of water

That lies in between......

The Snowman's Christmas

Once upon a time, in a village of ice and snow, there stood a snowman. Quite a distinguished gentleman, with a top hat, knitted scarf, and eyes of sparkling coal, he sat high above the hill and watched the people of the town each day. It stayed cold here all the time, and so his life was long and filled with years of memories. He watched children grow into adults with children of their own, all coming to play by his round body on the hill.

Each year brought the same excitement and sparkle to his village. Lights would twinkle everywhere, trees would sparkle like the icicles with tinsel that glittered, and people would hurry by with much to do on their minds. Over and over, he heard the word *Christmas*.

What is this Christmas he wondered to himself. How he wished he could move from his hill; how he wished he could slide down the hill on the sleds the children rode; how he wished he could spread his arms and legs and make what all the little ones called snow angels in the snow! But most of all, he wished to know what Christmas was. He knew it must be wonderful, for the entire village became kinder. His village was a very kind place to start, but at Christmas, that kindness grew even stronger with each smile and Merry Christmas greeting he heard each day.

But no one told him Merry Christmas. At night, he whispered it to the stars above. He whispered it to the moon, and he whispered it to the shadows of the snow angels he saw on the ground beside him. He whispered it to the giant fir trees that stood around him. "Merry Christmas, Moon! Merry Christmas, Stars!" One by one, he whispered it to all the trees around him. But no one wished it back.

In the moonlight, very tiny icicles rolled down his cheeks. In the stillness of the night, no one listened. But if they did, they might hear the softest of sobs coming from the hill.

Then, the quietest night came. It came each year. The houses sparkled, and all the parents and children were tucked inside early, waiting for Christmas to arrive. The sidewalks were empty, candles glowed in the windows, and church bells chimed.

Suddenly, on the hillside, something very magickal was happening. The shadows of little snow angels came to life and gathered around the snowman. They spread their glistening wings and wrapped them around his body. All at once, he felt himself lifting off the ground.

"What is happening?" he cried.

"Don't be afraid," they answered. "We are taking you to Christmas."

Before he could blink his shiny coal eyes, he was soaring through the moonlit sky, wrapped in the blanket of gossamer angel wings. He flew and flew, soaring high above the clouds, looking down on so many villages filled with lights. He saw other snowmen sleeping on the hillsides. He saw trees that looked a lot different from all the firs that grew beside him on the hill. He saw places where no snow lay on the ground.

Suddenly, he felt himself drifting downward. He closed his eyes in fear. Then, his body came to a soft landing on a bed of straw. Around him were animals he had never seen before. Each one said to him, "Merry Christmas!" This was the first time anyone had ever wished him a Merry Christmas.

"Hello, kind snowman. Merry Christmas!" brayed the donkey. "Hello, kind snowman. Merry Christmas!" mooed the cow. "Baahh! Kind snowman, Merry Christmas," bleated the lambs. Around a tiny baby, the snow angels clasped their wings in prayer.

It was very warm here, much too warm for a snowman, but the snowman wasn't melting. His heart, though, felt very, very strange. It was glowing like the lights of his village, for somehow, when his shiny coal eyes looked upon the baby, he suddenly knew the meaning of Christmas.

"Merry Christmas!" he whispered to the baby. And the baby laughed the sweetest laugh that melted the snowman's heart.

Fit for a Queen

T he woodlands were all abuzz. It was time for the annual Solstice festival. So much had to be done— honey gathered by the bees for mead, berries stomped on by the centipedes for berry wine, seed cakes baked by the squirrels, and decorations hung on all the wishing trees.

The Fairy Queen looked down at her closet in dismay. "Oh, I have nothing pretty enough to wear!" she cried. "I must make a proclamation. A contest to find the purest lace, the finest silk, shall be announced. The winner will be chosen on Solstice Eve."

The Fairy Kingdom filled with excitement. Word spread to all the spiders and worms, the expert lace weavers in the woodlands.

Little Penelope lived in the tall trees on the northern edge of the woodlands. She was a young spider, not having seen more than a couple of Solstice festivals. She didn't have any friends; the other spiders laughed at her and called her slow. A few of her spider eyes didn't see very well, and one of her legs was a bit shorter than the rest. Spinning webs was very hard for Penelope to do, but she loved to make her own designs in the high tree where no one could see.

The Queen's great oak was chosen as the contest site. All webs were to be spun on the oak, and judging by the Queen would take place at sunrise, Solstice Eve. Then, the winning lace would be quickly sewn by the Queen's expert seamstress, Wilhelmina Worm.

All the spiders filled out their entry forms and started spinning. The worms crawled up to the low branches and started spinning their lovely silk as well. When Penelope limped on her short leg to the entry table, the other spiders snickered in the branches.

"What does she think she is doing!?! Penelope, are you going to make a gown for the Queen?" they joked. "He he, wait until the Queen sees Penelope's creation!" they laughed in high-pitched spider giggles.

But Penelope ignored them. She slowly wrote her name. The print was very small, and Penelope had to focus all seven of her good eyes to see the lines. Her handwriting was crooked and uneven. The entry taker sneered. "You can't even write your name. How are you going to spin a web?"

Just then, the kind Fairy Queen was passing by in her carriage. She heard the entry taker and quickly stopped, taking hold of Penelope's entry form.

"Penelope, come with me. I will show you to your branch." And with a smile as bright as the Solstice Sun,

Penelope took the Fairy Queen's hand as she guided her to the oak branch.

"Everyone, good luck!" the Queen cried. "I shall be back on Solstice Eve morn to choose the lace for my gown."

The spiders spun smoothly and quickly, each layer of their webs perfect and precise. The worms chewed day and night, their constant munching annoying all the spiders. "Can't you keep that racket down!" the spiders yelled. "None of us can concentrate with all that chewing!"

Penelope sat by herself. She wasn't bothered by the worms' chewing; spinning was a place of comfort that led her into a world of her own. When she spun, she was happy.

The morning of the contest, busybody spiders crept from branch to branch, inspecting all the competition. When they reached Penelope's branch, the little spider held her breath and tried to think of calming thoughts. She knew how cruel the other spiders could be.

"Look at all those uneven edges!" they laughed. "Why, a grasshopper could spin a better web! It isn't even the right shape! You are just stupid, Penelope," they laughed.

Penelope brushed her tears away with her shortened leg. She was just about to tear her web apart when a kind whisper glided through the branches. It sounded just like her mother, but her mother had crossed to spider heaven the winter before. "It is beautiful, Penelope. The Fairy Queen will think so, too."

Penelope walked among the web, her little spider tears falling like dew drops on the lace. Her tears glistened like diamonds in the morning sun. Then, the sound of the Queen's trumpet blared in the woodlands.

"The Queen approaches," her squirrel footman announced. The beautiful carriage stopped at the base of the great oak. The Fairy Queen stretched her wings and flew from branch to branch, inspecting the work of every spider and worm.

"How lovely, what detailed work!" she cried. "What sharp angles, what pretty designs!"

Then, the Fairy Queen came to Penelope's web. Penelope held her breath. All the other spiders softly snickered in the tree. "Wait until she sees this one!" they giggled.

The morning sun was in the perfect spot. Penelope's teardrops glistened and shimmered.

"Oh," the Queen cried. "I have never seen such imagination and creativity; it is unlike any web I have ever seen, even in the lace-making Fairy Realms of Venice! There shall be no other gown in the entire Kingdom like it!"

And with that, she placed a lovely golden ribbon across Penelope's little chest.

Wilhelmina sewed all night, placing beads and crystals in the places Penelope's tears had sparkled, as the Fairy Queen had instructed. Penelope sat at the Queen's table at the Solstice Festival. Everyone who saw the Queen admired the beauty of her gown.

When the Festival was over, the Queen clasped Penelope's leg and asked her to live in the Castle as her gown designer. No one ever made fun or called Penelope stupid again.

School Bells

*E*liza lived in an old one room schoolhouse with her parents and little brothers. Each day, the family awakened to the ringing of the schoolhouse bell. "Hooray!" shouted Eliza. "It's time for school." She would run to the little hole in the wall at the far corner of the classroom and sit like the obedient student she was.

Her little brothers teased her. "Don't you know mice can't go to school?" they chided.

"I can, too, go to school," Eliza cried, grabbing her tiny notepad off the hook that Papa had made in the wall by her mouse hole. Papa took the ashes from the wood stove and put them into a tiny jar for Eliza to use as ink. He carved her the most beautiful wooden pen with his teeth. Her notepad was filled with letters and numbers and pretty, little hearts with the words "Miss Holly" inside.

Eliza loved Miss Holly. She was the prettiest teacher Eliza had ever seen, even if she had never seen another. At night, in the stillness, Eliza would climb up on her desk, hold her paper and pen in hand, and pretend she was the teacher.

Learning was easy for Eliza; she already knew her ABCs and was starting to add and subtract all the way up to one hundred! Papa said she was the smartest mouse he ever knew. Eliza offered to show her brothers, but they wanted no part of school and would much rather play and run in the fields all day long.

Then one day, a terrible thing happened. One of the students misbehaved and was told to stand in the corner.

"Eeeek!!!" he screamed. "Miss Holly, a mouse!"

"Quit joking, James, and stand quietly in the corner," Miss Holly scolded.

"But there's a mouse, Miss Holly………LOOK!!!"

Eliza tried to run fast enough, but the tip of her tail was showing.

"Now see what you have done," Papa yelled. "Now we must leave our warm home and find another!"

That night, Eliza packed her tiny notepad and with tears in her eyes followed Mama and Papa and her little brothers out into the fields. Before she went, she left the tiniest note on Miss Holly's desk. It said, *Thank you to the prettiest teacher in the world.*

The following morning, Miss Holly set her books down quickly at her desk. She was late this morning, with much to do before class began. She opened a window, and a gust of wind caused the tiny scrap of paper to flutter through the air. *I had better sweep the floors, in case there are any mouse droppings around*, she thought to herself. She swooshed her broom back and forth, catching a very tiny speck of paper in the dust. She swept it out the door, and the wind carried it off. She never knew the treasure written in tiny mouse strokes on that page.

Meanwhile, Mama and Papa mouse were beginning their new journey. They stayed the first few nights with distant cousins, and then Grandma and Grandpa's home. Grandma and Grandpa lived way across the town, quite a long journey for little mouse feet.

Everywhere they went, all the town mice marveled at Eliza's reading and mathematical skills. She counted grains of wheat and kernels of corn for them to share evenly. She wrote tiny mouse letters to deliver to other relatives along the way. She told them what all the words written on packages meant. She warned them which packages said words like "poison" and told them NEVER to eat from them.

Finally, Eliza's family found a cozy home in the town library. Eliza couldn't believe her eyes! There were shelves and shelves of books everywhere, more than one hundred. She would have to learn to count higher! There were letters posted on the wall and town announcements. It was a dream come true for the happy little mouse. There was a wood stove for Papa to collect the ashes, and there were stacks and stacks of paper, enough to write on each day.

Then, a wonderful thing happened. Soon, when the town church bell rang its chimes, little mice started walking up the back library steps. In a remote storage closet, amidst the dust and boxes, a pretty, little teacher by the name of Miss Eliza was holding class. She taught ABCs, mathematics, and many other subjects that she learned at night while climbing through the library bookshelves.

There were so many corners and cubbyholes in which to hide; the little mouse family could live safely here for the rest of their lives. And each day, class began promptly at the ringing of the church bell.

One morning, Eliza found a little treasure on the box that was her desk. One of her students, Mary Jane, had written little strokes on a piece of paper. The writing was scribbled, but Eliza could read these words...*Thank you to the prettiest teacher in the world.* A tiny heart with the words "Miss Eliza" inside was drawn at the side of the page.

Eliza carefully folded her treasure and put it inside her teacher's notepad. There, it would be safe forever.

She would have to hurry...the school bells were ringing.

Where He Lay

M argaret and James O'Brien never thought they would own a castle. But here they were, in Ireland, restoring the ruins and rubble of just such a place. They moved in about five years ago, restoring as much as funds would allow. At this rate, Margaret figured they would get about one third of the way done by the next half century.

Margaret believed in fairy folk and spirits. James scoffed at the nonsense of it all. Friends warned them of the ghosts that haunted ancient walls, but Margaret felt nothing harmful in all the time she spent at the castle. In fact, one spirit became a beautiful friend.

Margaret shared her home with two beautiful wolfhounds, Connor and Ian. They were brindle colored and born of the same litter three winters before. How Margaret loved them! They had free roam of the castle and grounds and brought joy to her heart each and every day. James worked hard; his free time was spent on restoration. Connor and Ian were Margaret's only company...until one sunny morning.

She looked out from her kitchen window and saw Connor and Ian tousling in the yard. But joining the fray was a lovely wheaten hound, his long fur blowing in the breeze.

Well, what do you make of that? Margaret thought to herself. *We have a guest.*

She ran to the back door, but when she opened it, the hound was gone. She looked all around the grounds, but not a trace of him could she see. Connor and Ian seemed to be looking, too. They stood erect, their eyes searching left and right. Margaret had a hard time calling them inside.

"Come, boys, sit by the hearth," she called. Wagging their long tails, Connor and Ian stepped inside, dragging muddy paws along with them, and settled with heavy sighs by the warmth of the fire. "I will go and get some warm milk," Margaret whispered lovingly.

Margaret warmed their milk on the stove and got two biscuits from the jar on the counter. She walked into the parlor and gasped, dropping the bowls of milk on the stone floor. There at the hearth, beside Connor and Ian, was the wheaten hound. All three of them looked up at Margaret. *How, why, where,* all tossed around inside her head. Suddenly, the hound just faded in the light of the hearth, and he was gone.

Margaret cleaned the mess, already being helped by Connor and Ian's thirsty tongues. They seemed little upset by this occurrence. *I just saw a ghost,* Margaret thought to herself. *And a dog ghost at that!*

• • •

Margaret said nothing to James, who would only laugh and call her wild with imagination. In the weeks that followed, Margaret would see him in the garden with the hounds. She would feel the brush of a third long tail go by her at nighttime. She would often place a third bowl of warm milk and a biscuit by his favorite resting place at the hearth. Always, he would quickly vanish when she came near.

As time went on, her ghost hound stayed longer, came closer, allowed his fur to be ever so lightly touched by his new mom. Never when James was near; always when the four of them had the castle all to themselves. "My beautiful Spirit Boy," Margaret would whisper to him, with just as much love in her heart as for Connor and Ian.

Years passed. Money problems eased a bit, and James thought restoration of the derelict stable might be a worthwhile project. They could open the castle to tours and have horses for guests to ride throughout the grounds. He hired several contractors who went to work clearing away the ruins of the former stable's foundation. They cleared the ground and carted off much of the dirt as they prepared the land.

Margaret hadn't seen her ghost hound in many days. She missed him. Connor and Ian missed him, too. Their noses lifted in the air, searching out his familiar scent. Filled with worry and unable to tell James why, tensions grew between them.

"I thought the stable would make you happy, Margaret," he yelled. "You always wished for horses. Now, not a day of happiness passes by in our home."

Margaret just quietly stared out the window. So distraught and so alone in her grief, Margaret sought the help of another. She went to see an old woman in the nearby town who knew much about the ways of spirits and fairy folk. She told her about the hound.

"Has anything changed about the castle?" she asked. Margaret shook her head. But then she answered, "We are building a new stable for horses."

"Did you disrupt the old ground?" she asked.

Margaret's heart sank. "Yes," she answered.

"You moved his bones. He is gone," the old woman muttered.

When Margaret got home, she asked James if he had found anything unusual in the excavation.

"Looking for Celtic treasure?" he smirked.

"Did you, James? This is important to me!" she answered.

"Nothing. Just some old bones, a deer or big dog or something. I told the contractor to get rid of them."

Margaret went to her room and cried. Her friend was gone, her beautiful Spirit Boy. How she hated James. She didn't care about a new stable or horses. She wanted her lovely wheaten hound.

The stable was finished, but it stood empty for two winters. Connor and Ian were nine years old now, no longer tousling in the yard. They spent their days by the warm hearth. Ian left one summer morning as Margaret stroked his fur. She looked into his gentle eyes and told him to go find his friend. With that, he took his last breath.

James buried Ian by the stables. Margaret and Connor visited each morning in the very early hours after sunrise, when James left for work.

Things had never been the same between Margaret and James; two worlds and two beliefs just could not be shared. He had his work, she her hounds and garden. What once was a bright future seemed to fade away as quickly as the shadow of a wheaten hound by the hearth once did.

One blustery, rainy day, Connor caught scent of a familiar smell on the wind. He raced as he had not done in quite a long time to the other side of the castle grounds. "Connor, come!" Margaret yelled, running to keep up with his long strides.

Then, she saw them. A brindle and a wheaten hound, running in the grass, sun shining on their fur. Soon, a third hound joined in the fun, although a little slower.

"Oh, Ian, you have come back, and you have found him!" she cried. Tears rolled down her face. "Come inside," she called. "Milk and biscuits are waiting!"

James came home that night to a different wife. "I think it time we got a couple of horses for the stable," she said. "And maybe open up the castle for riding tours."

Not long after, Connor joined his brothers. His grave lay next to Ian's behind the stables. Margaret laid flowers on both of their graves, plus on a third grave next to both of theirs. (Only once did James ask about the spot. "Oh, just a squirrel I found in my garden," she answered.)

Standing over the graves, Margaret whispered, "Though your bones are gone, your heart lives here with me and your brothers and will for the rest of my life. One day, we will all walk these grounds together, I promise. My Connor, my Ian, and my Spirit Boy."

The Rain

I am like the rain

Falling.......

Downward to the earth

Its drops to seep into the earth

While others fill the puddles and splash back into the air

To fly toward the clouds again

I fell yesterday

I slid down the stairs like rain down a hanging branch

Falling to the earth

In a summer storm of a cloudy afternoon

Now clouds of black and blue and green

Mark my side

Like a painter's palette

I wonder if in dying moments

One is falling

Some spirits in a storm seeping into the earth

Some spirits in a gaze of wonderment

Flying toward the clouds again

The Stairway of Wishes

Belinda lay in bed, her feverish head keeping her pillow damp. Another sunrise came and went. She lost track of the days and the sunrises. Today was an especially brilliant one. The light coming in through the bedroom window was so brilliant. Belinda closed her eyes.

No one was there to bring her a cool drink of water. No one was there to lay a wet cloth on her forehead. She had lost her mother several seasons past; now, she struggled to farm a barren patch of dirt and begged in the village for a few coins to buy bread. The struggles of life caught up with her, and her health diminished. Now, her raspy breaths came shallow and hard, and her mind floated in and out of consciousness.

Though sweating feverishly, Belinda felt chilled, and the morning sunlight comforted her face. Her eyes opened upon hearing a soothing voice. There, at the side of her bed, was the most beautiful woman. White wings draped across her shoulders, silken curls cascaded down her neck. But her eyes! They were the deepest blue Belinda had ever seen, with a kindness that shimmered.

"My child," she whispered. "Look out the window. Do you see it?"

Belinda opened her eyes wide and looked out the window. The sun was brilliant, but it did not hurt to look into anymore. Then, she saw it. A beautiful, winding stairway that seemed to continue into the clouds.

"That is the stairway of wishes," the beautiful Angel said. "Tell me your heart's desire, and you shall ascend into it."

Belinda was confused. Was she dreaming? Was this real? She couldn't know for sure; her thoughts felt so foggy. Belinda was a young girl. A hard life had taken her soft skin, her shiny hair, and her dreams of the future, but within her heart, they still resided.

"I wish for a beautiful castle, with music and dancing and princes and princesses!"

"Are you certain?" asked the Angel.

"Oh, yes," cried Belinda.

No sooner had she answered than she found herself on that stairway, climbing to the top. She followed the light to a brilliant room of gold. Fancy gowns glittered, and princesses' necks were bedazzled with sparkling jewels. Flowers were woven into upswept, shiny hairstyles, and handsome princes vied for the eyes of the ones with whom they wished to dance.

Belinda felt invisible. She was dressed in her ragged bedclothes, her unbrushed hair was matted down with feverish sweat, and she looked down upon her bare feet with dismay. No one looked at her; in fact, no one even knew she was there. Belinda ran to the light and started running down the stairs.

"What is wrong?" asked the Angel, appearing out of the clouds. "Did not your wish make you happy?"

Belinda cried. "I have no gown, no jewels, no golden slippers for my feet."

"Do you wish for these?" the Angel asked.

"Oh, yes," cried Belinda. "Then I will be happy!"

In the blink of an eye, Belinda was back in the ballroom. This time, all eyes shone upon her. A mirror on the wall reflected the image of a beautiful maiden. Her hair was styled and shining, her neck was covered in diamonds, and a glittery gown of blue matched the satin of her silken shoes. Belinda took a minute to realize the reflection was her own.

Lovely princesses walked past her, mumbling to themselves about who this new comer might be. Their eyes were filled with envy, not kindness like the Angel's. Handsome princes asked her to dance. Unfortunately, Belinda didn't know the steps. Soon, the other dancers were laughing and making fun of her clumsiness.

Belinda's eyes filled with tears. This was no place for her. She started to run toward the door again. She felt someone brush her shoulder. It was the Angel.

"You have used two wishes, Belinda, and still you are not happy. Be very wise this time; this is your last wish."

Belinda didn't hesitate to answer. "I wish to be home again with my mother."

The blue eyes of the Angel seemed to deepen in color. She grasped Belinda's hand and led her to the stairs. "Go home, my child," she whispered.

Belinda raced up the stairs toward the light. She entered and saw her mother's open arms waiting. There was a warm bed, a cool drink of water, and a cold cloth for her head. "Rest now. There is hot soup on the stove for when you awaken."

Belinda didn't awaken. At least, not on this earthly plane. She awakened into a place of love and comfort and kindness. She was home.

Sea Fairies

*D*eep within the depths of the sea, the sea fairies live. With mermaid tails and flying fish wings, they flutter through the waves so fast that no one can see them. Well, no one except other sea fairies. They make their homes in oyster shells, snail shells, and empty tortoise carapaces and dine on sautéed seaweed and saltwater taffy for dessert.

They speak the language of the sea. They hear the dolphins' clicks and the whales' song, and they communicate with all the language of the seven seas. They have their own special song, a pitch so high only other sea fairies can hear and understand.

Sea fairies are immortal. Once every hundred years, they choose a very special oyster shell to build a nest within and place a tiny egg. Each fairy egg has a luster so beautiful that those not of the sea call it a pearl. This precious little egg is hunted and stolen from the sea fairies and used to adorn the necks and ears and fingers of those who cannot breathe or fly within the sea.

But sea fairies are immortal. From within these pearls, their light is so luminous that it continues to shine right through the shell. That is why each pearl is so beautiful; inside, the tiny fairies wait. They wait for the day someone will toss them back to the sea and salt water. Then, with the coming and going of one full moon, they will break free from their shells and live eternally as fairies of the sea. And all the other sea fairies will be waiting and listening for their songs.

The Song of the Sea

Caroline was a ghost. She walked the Cornwall coast just before the sun came peeking over the horizon. She came as a foggy mist, billowing hair blowing in the wind, long, white gown touching the tide as she walked her lonely path each night.

Many a solitary fisherman had cast his eyes upon her. A trick of the fog perhaps? No, the hair, the nightdress, the determined footsteps placed in steady gait...she was real.

Records of the village showed a Caroline Keefe, lighthouse keeper's daughter, lost at sea one August night, 1876.

A terrible storm had blown across the Cornwall coast a similar summer night in 1871. Caroline's father was keeper of the light. A vessel had strayed too close to the rocky shore and crashed. Caroline raced out to the sea (along with her father) in her nightclothes to help the stranded and dying seamen as they washed ashore.

One seaman was recorded in the village documents as Silas Jakes, age 26 or thereabouts. His cause of death was listed as drowning. Caroline was at his side when he died. He was the most beautiful of men, with piercing, brown eyes and hair that hung wet around his shoulders. "Sing to me,

Caroline," he said. "Sing me a beautiful song for my final sea voyage."

It is written that Caroline had the voice of an angel. She sang in the village church choir and sang to all the birds that visited the Cornwall coast. That night, she sang a most beautiful song to soothe a dying heart. It is often said that love takes time to grow; however, some believe it can happen in an instant. For Caroline, an instant was all it took. More than Silas' life was lost that night, for Caroline's heart was drowned in sorrow, as well.

Caroline lived for five years after that, never once letting song leave her lips. It is said she could no longer bear the sound of music. The birds would call to her, but Caroline never answered. Cornwall's music was now the lonely sound of waves crashing the shore.

If one can die of a broken heart, then Caroline surely left this earth because of one. On a foggy night, very much like one that happened five summers before, a storm rose off the Cornwall coast. Caroline disappeared that night. No trace of her was ever found, except for a pair of satin slippers in the sand.

Soon after, villagers started seeing her walk the lonely coast, long hair flowing in the night winds. Some even heard the sweetest sound of a woman's voice, the lilting notes echoing in the wind. Her song reached out to the sea, reached out to find the love she never really knew, the love she could never forget.

For ten years, the Cornwall ghost of a young woman was seen walking this same path, over and over again. Then, one night, a pair of villagers walking home from the pub in the early morning hours spotted a misty figure bending over something in the rocks. They told of haunting music filling the foggy night. Townspeople said they were drunk.

After this encounter, no one ever saw the Cornwall ghost again. Perhaps Caroline and Silas' hearts have found one another again. One can hope they began a voyage of eternal love.

The Tree Spirit

Once, at the edge of an ancient, dark wood, a stately oak stood. Her bark was peeling, and her boughs were brittle and empty in places of leaves, but she was beautiful, oh so beautiful. Her roots stretched to the north, south, east, and west. Tendrils of ivy clung to her trunk and shoulders. Each morning, she raised her arms to the sun in praise; each evening, she lowered her leaves in reverence to the moon and stars.

One day, a curious little fox tapped his paw across her trunk and asked, "Wise Oak, do you know what lies beyond the edge of the woods? I am going to take a long journey there and see for myself what waits beyond the hills."

The Wise Oak smiled within herself. "Little Fox," she whispered, "what lies beyond sits under the same sun, under the same moon and stars, as we. Our woodland is beautiful and home; it is enough for me. Why is it not enough for you?"

"I have heard the ravens and the crows caw. They speak of wondrous things—towers in the sky, strange beings in battle, fields of endless wheat, and orchards filled with fruit. I am sick of the berry bushes here in the woodlands; I want to see and taste and hear all there is to find beyond the forest."

The Wise Oak shook her branches in the wind. "Little Fox, I am very old and very tall. I have seen things, and I have heard things. Not all is beautiful outside the woodlands."

"Oh, what do you know?" the fox replied. "You sound just like the stupid badgers and raccoons, always frightened of straying too far, always hiding in their burrows."

Wise Oak sighed. "Be safe, Little Fox," she whispered. From tall in the sky, she watched him on his journey across the woodlands. She watched as he grew smaller and smaller, a speck on the grass. Then, she watched him fade into nothing in the brilliant sun.

Days passed. Each day, Wise Oak searched the fields for Little Fox. The nights grew chilly, the morning rain was damp on her bark, and the wind made her shudder.

Weeks went by. The nights came earlier, and Wise Oak lowered her leaves sooner each evening. Some leaves lowered all the way to the ground around her now.

One snowy afternoon, a very tired Little Fox limped slowly through the mounds of icy stillness. He was thin and weary and longed for the comfort of home. Finally, he saw her. Wise Old Oak towered among all the other trees.

"I cannot wait to tell her," he thought to himself. "She was right. All that waits beyond the forest is not so beautiful. I wish I had listened to her; I wish I had even listened to the badgers and raccoons. They weren't the stupid ones. It was my own foolish mind. I should have never made fun of them."

Little Fox crawled to the woodland's edge. There, the badgers and raccoons shared what little food they had to give him strength. They gave him sips of stored honey to restore his energy. Little Fox thanked them and said he must be on his way to see the Wise Oak. He rushed off, taking little notice of the sadness in his friends' eyes.

"Wise Oak, Wise Oak, it is your friend, Fox," he cried. Wise Oak stood very still. Her branches were empty of leaves; her trunk was cold and covered in ice.

Little Fox climbed inside a hole in her trunk. "When I wake up, I will tell you all of my adventures, Wise Oak. You were right all along. How I wish I had listened to you."

From deep within her trunk, Wise Oak's heart smiled. Her body was now without life, but her spirit was still alive deep within. Her spirit contained all the wisdom and history of the woodlands. Now, her body contained a tiny friend who would sleep until the warming sun shone on his fur again. Now, her spirit could rest as well.

The Merchant of Venice

Marco Polo lived in a fine house on the Venetian Canal. All know his place in history. But very few (humans that is) know another's name. Mice around the globe know him; his travels are famous. Mousco Polo lived in the walls of Marco Polo's house. He knew all about the world, for he listened to Marco talk of silk routes and faraway places no one had traveled to before.

Mousco loved these stories. His mouse heart, though small, was brave and longed to see the world as well. Perhaps he should stow away in Marco's bag and see the world for himself? But no. Mousco wanted to journey alone, to prove to his family and every family in Venice what a brilliant explorer he could be. He wanted his name to be written in the history journals of mice.

The world was a large place for a man, an even larger place for a tiny mouse. Night after night, Mousco sat in his tiny room and pondered how he might explore each corner of it. When Marco was away, he traced his tiny paws along the globe in the explorer's study, dreaming of oceans and continents and treasures in faraway lands.

One day, while scampering along the canal, searching for bits of bread that visitors had left for the pigeons of St.

Mark's Square, Mousco spied a teacup floating in the canal. Suddenly, his mind filled with ideas and adventures.

Taking a long stick in between in teeth, Mousco leaned forward as far as his tiny body could reach and caught the teacup, dragging it to the edge of the canal. With all his strength, he pushed it to the door of Marco's house, then along the wall until he reached the crack in the stonework where he dwelled. Alas, the cup was too big to fit through! Mousco thought and thought. Finally, he pushed it into a corner of the flowerbox and covered it with dirt so no one would see it.

That night, Mousco crept very quietly through the house and into the moonlit streets of Venice. He was looking for explorer treasures! It was a good night—he found an abandoned Popsicle stick near the gelato shop and a crumpled napkin by the espresso café.

Tired from all the lugging back to Marco Polo's house, Mousco slept until the next moon rose over the island. Then, after raiding the kitchen of several spaghetti strands and biscotti crumbs, he ventured to the flowerbox. With energetic paws, he scooped the dirt out of the teacup and pushed it to the edge of the canal. With bits of twine he carried in his explorer's bag (Marco always carried an explorer's bag, and Mousco learned to be just like him), the tiny mouse fastened the Popsicle stick to the side of the teacup. He had taken a smidgeon of sealing wax from Marco Polo's desk; Marco would never miss it, and Mousco needed it to build his ship. The crumpled napkin served as the sail, fastened to the Popsicle mast.

There was a gentle breeze that night, and Mousco climbed aboard his ship and sailed down the canal. He sailed until the sun was almost up. Then, he hid the teacup ship in a tiny crevice in one of the canal bridges and went home to sleep.

But Mousco couldn't sleep! Oh, how he loved exploring. Oh, how he loved the breeze in his whiskers! His tiny paws ached from steering his ship, but Mousco's heart was soaring as high as his napkin sail. That afternoon, he bragged to all his friends about his adventures. Of course, they didn't believe him!

"So where's your ship, Mousco?" Mousco didn't want to reveal her location, since some of his friends might not be trustworthy. "Sure, it's hidden," they sneered. "Mousco Polo, the explorer," they joked and scurried along to the outdoor market to scavenge for lunch.

Mousco was undeterred by their ridicule. He would prove them wrong. That night, he crept to the bridge and found his vessel waiting in the darkness. Mousco steered her to the island of Burano. He gathered snippets of the finest lace to bring back to the mice of his community. He also carried off a tiny thimble from the seamstress' shop and dragged it into a bakery shop where a baker was creating the dough for morning cakes and cookies. He filled his thimble full of panettone dough and brought it back to the teacup. Soon, his teacup was filled with treasure.

As the sun rose, a weary mouse steered back to his home. The panettone baked in the warmth of the sun. The lace snippets made a soft pillow for his head, and the boat glided back toward the canal, his home. No one saw the tiny teacup—no one, that is, except the gang of mice friends watching along the canal.

"Look! It's Mousco!" they squeaked. Running along the water's edge, they followed the teacup until it came to a soft landing under the Bridge of Sighs.

Mousco climbed out to his waiting admirers. He brought the panettone back to his neighborhood for all the mice families to share. He gave the snippets of lace to his mother, aunts, and grandmothers to sew into beautiful bonnets and sweaters for the mice babies born that season. Glistening pieces of colored glass from the island of Murano were carefully placed in Mousco's explorer sack. So precious, these would only be displayed in mice homes during the Christmas holiday. One day, the most beautiful ruby-colored glass would be entwined into a band of golden silk (also pilfered from Marco's desk.) But it was for a good cause. It would adorn the finger of Mousco's bride, Periwinkle, on their wedding day.

Mousco became famous as the Merchant of Venice. From then on, his teacup made many, many voyages across the canals, always bringing something new back to his friends and family. Mousco's world was small in comparison to Marco Polo's, but to this tiny mouse, he was exploring the globe! And Mousco's son, Mousco Jr., would soon follow in his father's pawsteps.

Centuries later, written in very tiny leather bound journals, stands the history of Mousco Polo, the bravest of mice. Inquisitive little mice often run their paws along its pages, dreaming of sailing into the unknown world.

Longing for Home

nce upon a time, thousands of centuries ago, the earth and sky were quite different. Earth had two moons, one lush and green with woodlands, and one cavernous and mysterious with tunnels and secrets and dark, deep holes within her belly.

On Cirus, the woodland moon, lived many creatures. But the most magickal of all were her colony of rabbits. Rabbits on Cirus were immortal. They spoke the most beautiful of all languages and were respected as the wise ones of the moon. Nothing lived on Pietra, the other moon; it was too hostile to grow any food, and the winds and rains could chill a rabbit and any other being to the bone. A beautiful bridge connected the two moons, and twinkling stars perched above its rails to light the way for any brave or mischievous being who dared to traverse her path.

Comet was one such adventurous rabbit. He loved to explore Pietra's caves; within them were the most beautiful creations, some hanging from her ceilings, and some growing tall from her ground. He could dig deeper than all his friends and would burrow away deep within the belly of his moon. *His moon*, he thought to himself. He loved Pietra, almost as much as the little girl rabbit who usually raced by his side each and every day. Stella was beautiful, with large brown eyes that looked at Comet as if he was the most handsome rabbit in the Universe.

But storms were intensifying on Pietra. Comet's parents warned him to stay away from the bridge. He was to play close to home from now on. Scientist rabbits foretold of terrible danger; Pietra was soon to be no more! Soon, she would explode and fall to earth in fiery pieces.

"Oh, no," cried Comet. "Not MY moon!" he cried. He would have to go and save her, or at least save a piece of her!

That night, Comet crept out of his burrow and stole across the woodland fields. From the shadows of the bushes, a worried little girl watched her love. "I knew he would go," she cried. "I cannot let him go alone." Stella followed, far enough behind for Comet's strong, twitching nose not to detect her presence in the shadows.

Comet crossed the bridge, looking up at the twinkling stars with tears in his eyes. He scurried down his favorite cave and carefully broke off the most beautiful pieces of the strange things that grew from ceiling to floor and floor to ceiling. Such beautiful colors, such sparkling wonders! Comet would be their caretaker forever. He placed each piece inside his backpack.

Comet's nose twitched in the air. "Who's there?" he called. A huge pair of brown eyes emerged in the darkness. "Stella! You shouldn't have come! It is too dangerous!"

But before Stella could answer, a terrible rumbling shook the ground. She hopped over to Comet, and he put his paw around her. "Don't worry Stella, I will keep you safe." But Comet couldn't keep them safe. A huge explosion rocked Pietra. Rocks and boulders began to fall around them. The beautiful, sparkling treasures started to crack and fall. Soon, Comet and Stella felt like they were tumbling too...faster and faster, tumbling down, down, down. The massive wall of boulders and rock shielded them, saved their lives. They stopped tumbling with a huge THUD.

"Are you okay, Stella?" asked Comet worriedly.

"I am okay, Comet. Are you?"

"Not a scratch," the brave bunny answered, though his body was bruised and sore all over.

Peeking through the boulders, Comet saw a strange sight. A luminous light glowed in the night sky. It was different from the one he was used to watching from his bedroom window. This was round and yellow, glowing like his father's lantern.

Comet and Stella climbed through the tiny openings and looked around. This wasn't Pietra; this wasn't home. Where were they?

There wasn't life here. There was, however, a lot of burning and destruction. Something terrible had happened here. Then Comet realized...his moon had fallen, and fallen

HERE. Earth. This was Earth, the place his rabbit eyes gazed upon each night before he closed them into sleep.

The beautiful light in the sky was HOME. Cirus—how could he ever find his way home again to her! Oh, how angry his parents must be, and how worried Stella's mother and father must be! And it was all his fault!

Stella began to cry. Tears rolled down her pretty rabbit cheeks.

"Don't cry, Stella, for I will keep you safe forever," promised Comet. And so, the two of them journeyed on, finding whatever bits of food that remained in a land scarred by a devastating collision.

Cirus rabbits were immortal. But the air on Earth is different; the magickal properties of home no longer kept Comet and Stella from aging. Time crept upon them.

They traveled to distant places far from the destruction, woodlands just as beautiful as home and filled with many beings. Some looked like them, but they didn't speak the same words. They didn't know the same magick of the moons. No one knew the ancient ways here; none spoke the language of the elders on Cirus. But the loving pair had each other, and their bond for one another grew stronger with each season, though their longing for home never ceased.

Stella and Comet kept their beautiful words and voices silent, except in the dark night moments when they gazed at their home in the star-filled sky. They wished for a starlit bridge to connect their bodies, for their hearts never lost connection for all they had lost. They stretched their tiny ears each night, straining to hear a voice from home. And, little by little, their ears grew longer and longer.

They practiced hopping higher and higher every day. Their legs grew bigger and faster, and their feet lengthened with each passing season, but never enough to hop home! Together, they raised a family of little ones who had never seen home. But Stella and Comet told them of the old ways, of the ancient magick, of the beautiful night sky with two moons and a bridge that connected their worlds.

Their children inherited the strange characteristics that had altered the appearance of their parents. Born with huge ears and long feet, their noses twitched with excitement as their father told them stories of Pietra and home.

Deep within the cavernous hole where they first landed, bits of crystal that Comet had placed in his backpack grew and flourished, bringing treasures of home to this place of Earth. Now they lengthened from floor to ceiling and from ceiling to floor, sparkling in beautiful shades of every color of Comet's home.

Still, to this day, on moonlight nights deep within the woodlands of Earth, one can see the shadows of Comet and Stella's children, the hares of the forest, stretching their long ears toward home. They listen for the sound of a familiar voice, calling for her long lost children in the night. Their strong legs hop as if they were trying to reach the moon. Perhaps they are.

Monsters in the Woods

A midst the bracken and brambles of an ancient forest lived a village of tiny fairies. Kind to all in the forest, the fairies helped anyone who called upon their twinkling lantern door lights.

One summer's eve, a baby opossum raised his tiny paw and knocked on the fairy door of a large birch tree. "Please help me," he cried. "My mama has been hurt. She is lying quite still at the forest edge."

Now the fairies knew never to go farther than the stream that bordered their woods. The edge of the forest was a place of danger, a place of monsters. But the little white opossum's mournful plea moved their hearts, so off several of the elder fairies went, with the baby following close behind.

It was hard to see in the dark. The firefly lanterns lit only a few feet of the path ahead. There were briars and thorns and masses of ivy tangling the ground.

"Please hurry," cried the little opossum. "She was so still," he said, weeping through whispered words.

"How was she hurt?" asked Blackthorn fairy.

"All at once, we heard a very loud noise coming toward us in the middle of the road. Mama cried for all of us to climb into her pouch. Then, we heard a very loud thump, and mama stopped moving."

"You mean there are others?" asked Blackthorn fairy.

"Yes," answered the little opossum. "My two sisters and my three brothers, they are all much tinier than me. Only I had the strength to seek help."

Blackthorn fairy whispered to his friend, Mistletoe. "I fear what we find will not be good," he sighed.

"We must try," answered Mistletoe, trying to sound as hopeful as possible because she knew the little opossum was listening.

"This way!" the little opossum cried. "See that tall pine tree? I remember it. It was here!"

The fireflies left the lanterns and flew ahead, buzzing around a very still body at the edge of the road. They shone while the fairies looked at Mama Opossum. They looked at her eyes, half closed in sleep. They listened to her heartbeat with tiny acorn halves place upon her chest. They climbed up inside her deep pouch and found the babies, all tucked safely inside.

"Is mama all right?" asked the little opossum.

"She must rest. She is in shock," answered Blackthorn fairy. "We must get help before the day begins."

With that, the fairies took out silver flutes. They played a high-pitched melody. Soon, the lights of shining eyes appeared among the trees. Mr. Fox came first. Then, a large raccoon with a baby by her side. Finally, a swift brown hare ran out from behind the trees.

"You called for us?" they asked.

"Yes, please help us. We need to move her before the sun rises and monsters start to cross the road. One of them hurt her this night. She needs to rest in the safety of the trees before the monsters come again and find us!"

Gently, Mr. Fox and Mama Raccoon took hold of Mama Opossum. They slowly moved her body to the safety of the pine trees.

"Thank you," said Blackthorn fairy. "Time will tell if she will be all right."

The elder fairies gathered the night nectar of moonflowers into seedpods and slowly poured drops into Mama Opossum's mouth. They mixed a salve of willow bark for her bleeding paw. Meanwhile, Mistletoe searched the morning dew for sweet water to soothe the crying, hungry babies. Little Opossum helped feed them.

At midday, Mama Opossum opened her eyes wide. The fairies told her of the bravery of her son. Mama Opossum was very sore, but it seems only a paw was injured badly. Mistletoe wrapped it in the soothing leaves of ivy and tied it to Mama's leg with a tall fern frond. Blackthorn Fairy made a walking stick out of an oak branch.

Together, this strange band of friends walked very slowly back to the fairy village. Mistletoe and Blackthorn weren't used to such journeys. When near collapse themselves, the two of them and the other elders climbed into the coolness of Mama Opossum's pouch. They told fairy stories to the babies and to brave Little Opossum.

"One day, when you are full grown, we should like your help, Little Opossum," Blackthorn fairy requested. "Only the bravest beings of the forest learn the song of our flute. You will become one of us, helping those in need."

Little Opossum's chest swelled to twice its size. Mama Opossum listened, smiling with pride, but worrying with a mother's heart at the same time. There were monsters at the edge of the forest, she thought to herself. She met one last night. But she also knew it was her tiny son's courage that saved her and his siblings. Without him, they surely would have perished.

At that very moment, several miles away, a village wagon passed the site of the large pines at the edge of the woods.

"Daddy, is this where it happened?" two little voices asked. "Can we see if she is all right?"

The father stopped his wagon, and the three of them got out. There was no body by the roadside.

• • •

"She must be okay," he said with relief in his voice. "C'mon, back in the wagon now, you two. You know there are monsters in the woods."

"Yes, Papa," they whispered.

Sand Castles

arlan Jacobs loved the sea. He was a native Islander, one of those staunch New Englanders who saw more Nor'easters than they could remember blow their way. Being Harlan was now 86, that was quite a bit. He worked in the fishing industry, but now, too old to set sail, his days were spent on sand.

Building things—that's what Harlan loved best. And storytelling. Put the two together, and one Island senior met each day with a smile.

Harlan built sand castles now. He could replicate the village right down to its cobbled streets and flower box blooms. He could create a dragon or a whale with the sculpt of a mound of sand, and thus he could widen the eyes of any child to saucer size.

Tourists sat for hours listening to his seafaring tales, the history of the Island, the keeper's light, and the sea captains of centuries past. Everyone on the Island knew the place to find Harlan was the sea, or as close to it as physically possible nowadays.

Beach guides drove up and down the coastline, making sure all was safe. They commented on Harlan's presence.

"Look at that crazy old man. He spends all day building something that vanishes with the night," Adam, the young tour guide hired for the summer season, sneered.

"Oh, I don't think you're right," his partner replied. "Harlan's work won't vanish."

Adam's partner was a native Islander. He had grown up listening to the old man's tales and witnessed the sand scenes that accompanied his stories.

Adam fired back, "Then maybe you're as crazy as he is. Maybe it's the Island air."

A group of children sat around Harlan as yet another huge vessel was created. There were sailors on deck, an anchor on the side, and masts of a folded sail perfectly in place. As they sat entranced, seals swam by, gulls flew overhead, crabs foraged in the sand, and biting black flies continued to be an annoyance. The sea, Harlan's home. He shared with all who lent an ear to listen.

Day after day, each summer season for years and years since his retirement, Harlan let the seawater soothe his arthritic hands as they formed each corner of a masterpiece. His hands were slower, and his legs hurt walking to and fro to gather water for his art, but that couldn't deter the spirit of a man and his purpose.

One night, Harlan went to sleep and didn't wake up to the call of the gulls. His spot on the sand lay undisturbed for

• • •

the first time in many a summer season. The seals swam by, the sea birds cried overhead, the crabs and flies were busy looking for something to bite, but an empty space filled the coast.

Tourists staying for the summer season appeared on time, as usual. "Where's Harlan?" the children asked.

The tour guides explained that Harlan was now fishing in a peaceful sea. It was hard to tell who was the most upset, the little children waiting for their tales of whales and dragons, or their parents who had grown up listening to the same imaginings of an old man and his sea. The salt of tears added to the ocean supply that day.

One tour guide whispered softly to himself as he watched the sorrowful day unfold. People kept coming, asking for their friend, staring down at the leveled sand and the castles waiting to be imagined. *Yeah, I don't think you were right Adam...not at all.*

Some things vanish with the tide, but some remain forever. And if it is true that spirits linger in the places their hearts truly belonged, then Harlan remains with the sand and the sea.

The Blizzard

O nce upon a time, a story was told to grandparents and parents and retold to each generation that followed. It is the story of a great snowstorm, a blizzard like none seen before or since. It covered the trunks of stately trees, it swallowed up the entrances to all the rabbit warrens, it filled up the fox dens, and it swept into the bear caves with each gust of wind. The sky was blinding; the paths disappeared; all seeds and berries and water disappeared under layers and layers of snow.

What would or could be done? Where would all the animals find shelter in the storm?

Now, fairies lived in this land as well. They were tiny, the size of a pinky finger, and they seldom showed their faces to anyone, including the animals in the forest. But the fairies were watching the snow, too; they saw all the animals and their families struggling to keep warm and dry. They knew what they must do—it is decreed in fairy law that all the beings of the woodlands must be kept safe.

Hidden in the hillside were huge fairy mounds. These were places upon which no human ever trespassed. The fairies guarded the entrances with magickal spells, feared by all who knew the fairy lore.

The king of the fairies held a great meeting in the mound. He announced, "We shall open it for them."

The fairies gasped. Never had they opened the door to their magickal mounds—not to hare, fox, owl, bear, or any animal of the woods or sky.

"It is decreed! We must begin now; they are freezing out there!"

And begin they did. The fairies visited each den, each warren, each tree stump, and each crevice in the cairn where mouse and bird were hiding. They darted among the falling snow, fluttering their glistening wings and shaking the flakes off as they went on their mission. "Come, we will give you shelter," they told each animal.

And each one followed. They came to the great mounds and were sheltered inside until the great blizzard was over. The foxes, the owls, the bears, the rabbits, the mice, the hawks, the wild hounds, and the horses all came and dwelled in peace. There were berries and seeds and nuts and nectars, enough for all to share.

From then on, the fairy folk and the woodland beings of the forest and sky have bonded in friendship. Together, they guard the sacred mounds and keep them safe from harm. A friendship pact throughout the ancient land was written in the stone of the fairy mounds that day, never to be forgotten.

The beings of the woodlands and the fairies have always remained friends and play in secret corners of the forest away from human eyes. Foxes and bears tell their cubs, owls tell their owlets, hounds tell their puppies, and all fairies tell their little ones this tale. It is decreed by the fairy king's great-great-great-great-great-grandson, who rules this very day.

Within the fairy mounds, his ancestors lay in peace. Those who respect the wee folk know to let them remain at rest, never disturbing their sacred ground. No being of the woodlands will ever disrespect the mounds and the fairy folk who kept them safe from harm....

And, should a blizzard come their way again, the fairies will be waiting to welcome them all home within the mounds again. That ancient snow has long since melted, but the words in stone will last forever, and forever shall the fairies and the woodland beings remain friends.

The Blue Scarf

They said good-bye at the train station that morning, making promises that fate could only determine keeping. Mary was young, beautiful, and naïve. Jack was handsome, roguish, and full of excitement about going to war.

"You promise to write me every night, Jack," her eyes focused directly into his.

"I promise, Mary, every night."

So young, so foolish, each not having the slightest inkling of what lay in store for both of them.

"Here, take this," she whispered. She untied the delicate, blue lace scarf around her neck and handed it to Jack.

"Now, I don't think this is military issue, Mary," he laughed, with a twinkle in his eye.

"You take it and carry it with you always. It is my good luck charm, filled with love."

Jack stuffed the scarf into his pocket and grimaced. "I will never hear the end of it if the others see me with this," he added.

Mary, Mary eyes of blue
I promise I'll come home to you...

Everyone in Jack's regiment knew about that scarf. "See this? My Mary has eyes as blue as this scarf, as blue as a summer sky." He held it every night. It was his beacon, like a lighthouse light beckoning the way home. That piece of lace meant more to him than his rations for the day. He took it with him always, in march and in battle. He sang that refrain before each battle; it became his mantra of hope, of courage:

Mary, Mary eyes of blue
I promise I'll come home to you...

Jack did write to Mary as promised, each night in the beginning. But letters and time grew sparser and sparser, and too much death and suffering seals a man's emotions tight within his heart. Jack couldn't share such burdens with Mary, and small talk seemed so unimportant these days.

Mary wrote. Sometimes her letters came daily. Other times, mail was slow and backed up, and a pile of her notes came all in the same day.

Even with words unspoken or unwritten, Jack and Mary's love never wavered.

Then, news of a battle up north came to Mary's town. A large battle of converging armies fought in a little town in Pennsylvania. Mary was a few hundred miles away in New Jersey, not so near a distance back then. But it was closer to home than Jack had been in over a year. The news of the battle was grave; so many had died. Tales of soldiers lying in the July heat, wounded and dead, horrified Mary. She had not heard from Jack...was he safe?

She scoured the newspaper clippings. They spoke of people rummaging the battlefield for items of monetary worth or battle souvenirs.

"Father, I am going."

Mary's father tried to dissuade her, but there was no letting in, so he and his daughter took off in his carriage for a town several hundred miles away. Mary's father sought to keep her hopes high, but the news was more and more horrific as they neared the small town. And when they got within wind range, the smell was unlike anything they both might have imagined.

"This was a mistake, Mary. I should never have agreed to this."

"Please, father, someone must know where he is."

Mary inquired in town at the hospital for news of Jack's whereabouts. No one could say, except that his regiment had suffered severe casualties.

The town was in complete disarray; the number of bodies was overwhelming, too many to be buried. Dead animals lay where they had succumbed to bullets and cannon fire.

One kind soldier with a bandage around his head stepped over to Mary and her father. "I heard you talking to the doctor. I was with Jack up at Little Round Top. So many fell about me, I do not know if Jack was one of them."

Mary looked into the soldier's eyes with eyes that pleaded for more.

"Thank you, sir," Mary's father replied, with weariness in his eyes and fear in his heart. "Where is this Little Round Top?" her father asked.

Within moments, Mary was running in the direction of the soldier's pointed finger. She ran until she could hardly breathe, exhaustion overwhelming her tired body.

"They really are as blue," the soldier whispered to himself.

"What?" asked Mary's father.

"Um....nothing. Hope you find him, sir. May God go with you."

Mary ran until her eyes could not tell one soldier on the ground from the next, her mind in a haze of disbelief. Then, she saw it—her lace scarf, blood obliterating its former sky blue color, clutched in the hand of a disfigured and bloated corpse.

The summer heat and the agony of death change a person's appearance; a soldier's own mother would have had difficulty recognizing any of these boys. But Mary knew. She identified his body. An unfinished letter was found inside his coat pocket, addressed to Mary Cooper, Princeton, New Jersey.

"I will take you home, my Jack. I promise," she whispered as she gently lifted the scarf from his hands and placed it inside the pocket of her skirt.

Jack's body traveled in the carriage with Mary and her father. His remains were placed on a peaceful hillside. Mary planted blue forget-me-nots on his grave.

Mary did marry. It seems that the young soldier with the bandage around his head came from a nearby New Jersey town. He just couldn't get those blue eyes out of his head. Almost two years later, he journeyed to Princeton, seeking out his blue-eyed princess.

Together, they had five children, the youngest of whom had the bluest eyes and a roguish twinkle in his eye. His name? Well, I guess I need not have to tell you that.

Tree Rings

The Fourth of July race was announced. This year, the Centerville Ants would race against the Pineview Spiders.

Lewis lived in Centerville with his family. There was his sister, Amelia Ant, his parents, and, of course, his pet flea, Freddie. Lewis had been sickly since birth. Now, at six years old, he spent most days in bed snuggled next to Freddie. By now, most ants his age could push at least ten times their weight in breadcrumbs or sugar grains, but Lewis didn't have the strength of the others. He was well liked, though; there were always friends dropping by the ant hole to see him and tell him the Centerville news.

"A race?!" Lewis shouted. "How I wish I could be in the race! Please, Mama?" he pleaded.

"Now Lewis, you know what the doctor said. You must rest," she lovingly replied.

"Aw, Mom." Lewis shrugged his little ant shoulders.

"Sorry, Lewis. Maybe you could come and watch," his friends shouted as they hurried out the door.

"Could I, Mom? Could I???"

Lewis' mom and dad loved him with all their hearts; it was hard to refuse anything their tiny son wished. So, on the morning of the race, Lewis and Amelia dressed very warmly.

Even though it was July, Mama Ant always made sure they had their hats on and sweaters tied around their shoulders in case of a chill. Papa Ant carried Lewis on his shoulders; he was very strong.

Soon, they made it to the race site. A huge tree stump near the boundary of Centerville and Pineview formed the track. The ants had constructed a ramp to climb the tall sides. The spiders sat on the twig benches on the sidelines, waiting for the signal for the race to commence.

"Please, Papa, can you carry me up the ramp?" Lewis asked. Papa lifted him high upon his shoulders and carried him to the top of the tree stump.

Lewis' eyes opened very wide. "Papa, what are all those rings?" he asked.

"They tell the tree's story," his papa replied. "Each ring marks a year in the tree's life, for all to see. Some are wider than others, strong and sure, for when the tree was healthy. Some are narrower and weaker than the other years, but the tree lived on and grew strong again. If you count the rings, you can know how long the tree has lived."

"I am like the narrow ones, Papa, aren't I?" the little ant whispered.

Papa tried to keep his voice very strong and steady. "Yes, but you will grow strong and steady again, too, my son."

The ants and spiders were lining up at the starting line. The spiders were a rowdy bunch, egging on the ants and telling them they would eat their spider dust. Lewis' friends saw their friend, high upon his Papa's shoulders. "Good luck, guys," the little ant yelled.

There were whispers among the ant team. They had decided something very, very important. The team captain whispered into Papa Ant's ear. Papa called Mama and Amelia.

"Lewis is joining the race!" Papa cried.

"WHAT???" Mama Ant screeched.

"Don't worry, Mama. It's all right."

"I am in the race, too," Papa answered.

"Now both of you have gone insane!" Mama shouted.

The spiders and ants formed their positions. Papa Ant held Lewis on his shoulders at the head of the line. Bang! The signal rang out, and the race began.

Slowly, the team of ants pushed Papa and Lewis around the track. The spiders whizzed by on their eight legs, a bit confused as to what was happening. All spider eyes stared at the strange occurrence. Their opponents were purposely losing the race, just to let a weak little ant join the fun.

At once, the spider team captain shouted, "Slow down!" The spiders stopped running; they crept at a snail's pace along the rings, barely moving any of their eight legs.

"What kind of a race is this?" some of the spectators jeered. But soon, more started cheering and yelling Lewis' name. "Lew-is, Lew-is, Lew-is," the crowd roared.

Rounding the final ring, Papa and Lewis led the winning team across the finish line.

"Congratulations," the spider team captain said, as he extended one of his hairy legs to Papa Ant.

"We won, Papa, we REALLY won!!!" Lewis shouted.

There was a big picnic after the race. The spiders were all invited, in gratitude for what they had done for Lewis. Papa, Mama, Amelia, and especially Lewis were the guests of honor.

Lewis felt very tired, and the family left the picnic early so he could get some rest. But Lewis didn't rest. He told Freddie the whole story before he closed his eyes (when the moon rose in the sky).

Lewis' rings of life were very short. The coming winter left him very frail, and by spring of the following year, his little heart lost its strength.

But Lewis was remembered always. Each Fourth of July, the tree ring race was held. It was called Lewis' Race from that first summer without him. Spiders gathered each year to spin beautiful rings, one for each year of Lewis' short life. They spin each one beautiful and strong, for that is what their brave little teammate was.

• • •

As a side note: Amelia began practicing gymnastics every day with Freddie. Mama was fearful she might suffer a concussion or broken leg, but Papa said that it was her time to race, and so she did. The following summer, Amelia took first place in the state finals for the high jump.

The Journey

Peggy, Miranda, and Beth were traveling out west alone for the very first time. The year was 1871. The sisters boarded the railway car to visit their grandparents; they hadn't seen them in fifteen years. Now, grown up enough to make the long journey alone, their anticipation couldn't have been greater.

Beth was the youngest, only 18. Peggy and Miranda were in their early twenties. Peggy was a talented horsewoman; she loved riding. Miranda was the quietest of the three, preferring to sit home sewing with her beloved cats at her feet. Beth was the beauty, expected to make quite a handsome catch of a husband one day soon.

"Watch over your little sister," their mama had said, with just a twinge of worry in her voice.

"We will, Mama. Don't worry," they laughed.

And so it began. New faces, new sights, new smells, a new something each and every day. Nearly three-quarters of the way to their destination, the terrain changed from the prairies to the mountains of the West. The sisters held their breath as the train rumbled across bridges over rushing water.

The most frightening, though, were the tunnels. They hated the tunnels. The sisters closed their eyes and waited until they were sure daylight streamed through the rail car windows again.

Peggy and Miranda opened their eyes to brilliant sunshine. The train had stopped, and the scenery was so beautiful that they decided to step down from the train and walk about to stretch their legs. It was unlike anything they had ever seen.

"So beautiful," gasped Peggy. "Look!" Wild ponies raced across the northern landscape. "Oh, they are the most beautiful horses I have ever seen!"

Colorful blossoms dotted the land. Smells of honeysuckle and jasmine filled the air. The sky held no clouds, its blue the deepest hue the girls had ever seen.

"Where's Beth?" asked Miranda.

"Oh, she must be flirting with one of the young passengers," Peggy answered.

Just then, the softest cat curled its tail around Miranda's legs. "Oh, aren't you the dearest little one!" she exclaimed, scooping him up into her arms.

"Something is wrong, Miranda. Where is the train?"

"Have we walked that far?" Miranda replied, for the first time feeling a sense that something wasn't right.

Just then, a lovely young woman seemed to appear out of nowhere. "You must choose," she said.

"Choose?" Peggy asked.

"Yes, come with me," the young woman responded. "I will show you."

In an instant, though they hadn't lifted a foot, they were back inside the tunnel. Smells of burning embers filled the air, and smoke filled the tunnel. Their train lay in a tangled heap of metal off the tracks.

"Beth!!" they screamed. Stepping over rubble, the sisters climbed on top of twisted passenger seats and broken windows until they found her. She was lying very still with her eyes closed.

"You must decide which journey to take," the young woman whispered. "You can stay with your sister, or you can leave the tunnel and journey with me into the beautiful land you glimpsed just moments before."

"We cannot leave her; we promised Mama," said Peggy. Her thoughts roamed to the wild horses as she said the words.

Miranda thought of the precious kitten waiting. She nodded her head. "Yes, we cannot leave."

The young woman waved farewell and disappeared through the light at the tunnel exit. Peggy and Miranda opened their eyes. Peggy couldn't move; she couldn't feel her legs. Miranda could not see; a burning pain shot across her face and chest. Beth held both their hands until help arrived, though dizzy and dazed herself.

Beth suffered a slight concussion but recovered quickly. Peggy and Miranda, unfortunately, suffered serious injuries that day. The elder sisters would spend the next eight years sealed away in their parents' Victorian home. Peggy was paralyzed, a wheelchair, not a saddle, for her seat now. Miranda suffered irreparable damage to her eyes; she was blind.

Beth married a handsome banker two years after the accident. Her sisters did not fare so happily, however. The two seemed to be mad at the world. They never smiled, and they never joined society again. Peggy painted wonderful scenes of handsome, wild horses running amidst colored blossoms in the hills. Miranda sat at the window, staring at a world inside her mind, her cats curled in her lap.

Peggy died May 7, 1879 at 2:45 in the afternoon. Exactly thirty minutes later, Miranda journeyed to join her. Upon finding the bodies, all expressed the same words...*In the past eight years, never have we seen such smiles of contentment upon either of their faces.*

An unfinished painting sat upon Peggy's drawing desk. It was of a beautiful woman standing before the entrance of a long, dark tunnel...

Old Joe

Old Joe was a cemetery dog, a stray who roamed among the graves in the quiet acreage of a town burial place. He was an ordinary dog, brown, fluffy tail, droopy ears, the kind most pass by in shelter cages. But Joe was loved.

Mrs. Harris, Plot #23, Row 15. Joe visited her each night around seven for his biscuits. Mrs. Harris was a lonely, old ghost—before Joe, that is. He gave her a reason to roam across town and grab some dog treats off the general store shelf without anyone ever being the wiser about it.

There was Mr. Jenkins. Old Joe loved the grumpy, old man. He always pretended to holler about Joe coming by, but Joe and everyone else knew it was just hot air coming out of his ghostly mouth. His hugs were warm and loving.

There was also Billy Swenson, the teenager in Plot #51, Row 11. He said Joe looked a lot like his dog, Ranger. He missed Ranger a lot—before Joe, that is.

Joe made his rounds each night, like an intern in residency, bringing a different kind of medicine to the spirits of forgotten ghosts. Joe was a scrappy survivor, but visitors to the cemetery—human visitors that is—started noticing the mangy-looking mutt wandering about. That's what they called him "Mangy Mutt," not Old Joe, his real name.

One morning, a truck drove into the cemetery. It wasn't the usual caretaker's truck. Billy Swenson saw it. He saw a man come after Joe with a long pole and put a rope around his neck. He threw Joe in the back of his truck and slammed the door hard behind him.

Billy told the other cemetery residents. Mrs. Harris cried that evening, especially when biscuit time came around. Grumpy Mr. Jenkins revealed his loving heart when he didn't even have the spirit to moan and groan anymore.

Billy took it the hardest. Losing Joe was like being separated from Ranger all over again. What could they do? Nothing it seemed.

The cemetery became a very lonely place over the next few days. With Joe, there was love and barks and reasons to get up and roam around. Without him, there was endless rest and time to dwell on being forgotten by family members who never visited anymore.

Joe found himself in a cold, dirty cage. Other dogs surrounded him, barking, shaking, and growling.

"He's a friendly, old boy. Not much to look at, though," he heard a man say as he walked by.

My name is Joe, the frightened dog thought to himself. *Mrs. Harris says I am handsome.*

"We don't have much choice; poor boy's time is up." They came for Joe around 11 that morning, leading him to a back room and placing him on a table. Joe didn't remember much after that, except that he got very sleepy.

When he woke, he found himself lying in the warm grass, behind Plot #51, Row 11. "Joe, Joe, you've come back!" cried Billy. The boy hugged Joe and knew. "Joe, you're one of us now. They can't see you. They won't chase you away ever again!"

Billy told the others. Mrs. Harris gave Joe about a hundred spirit kisses. They felt different now, like little wisps of wind. Mr. Jenkins didn't complain once that day.

Old Joe was home to stay. He might have been a stray, but he always had a home. After all, what is a home? A place where others love and need you and call you by your name. It didn't matter if they were living or deceased.

Be My Valentine

It was nearly February 14, and Forrest Squirrel had no heart to give to his lady, Corinne. What could he do? Snow was on the ground, and seeds and nuts were not plentiful enough to form a Valentine for the one he loved.

Corinne was so beautiful, and out of all the other squirrels, she had chosen *him* to be her Valentine. He had to give her something really special for this very special day. He asked his friends, "What do you think would be a nice gift for Corinne?"

William Fox answered slyly, "Wow, are you in big trouble if you don't find something soon!" Forrest's little squirrel mouth turned upside down, and his eyes looked upon the frozen ground.

"Don't you have enough seeds stored away to make a little heart wreath?" Danny Chipmunk asked.

"No, I was too busy catching the eye of Corinne to catch a big stash for the winter," Forrest sadly answered. "I don't know what I am going to do," he added with a sigh.

"Ask Mother Rose," said Jimmy Badger.

"She is sleeping now," answered Forrest. "She won't like being disturbed."

"Go ahead, ask her," the badger urged. "She knows EVERYTHING."

Forrest walked slowly up to Mother Rose and tapped her thorny branches.

"Who is it?" Mother Rose sharply asked.

"It is Forrest, Mother Rose. I need your help. I have nothing to give my Corinne, and Valentine's Day is tomorrow! I have to get her something so special. Please help me, Mother Rose."

"Hmmmmmmmm," Mother Rose sighed. "You know I do not like being awakened before spring. It took great courage to tap my branch! You must really love this little squirrel."

"Oh, I do!" Forrest answered. "She is the most beautiful squirrel in the whole woodlands, Mother Rose, just as beautiful as each of your roses. Please, Mother Rose, tell me what to do," the little squirrel pleaded.

Mother Rose felt her sleeping heart stir this snowy morning. It had been so many long winters since someone had said something so beautiful to her. "Come to me the moment the sun rises tomorrow. Do not delay; you must be here on time. I will have your answer then. Now leave me. I have need of much rest."

Forrest walked home, still worried about tomorrow but believing Mother Rose. He hardly slept a moment all night. At the first glimmer of sunlight, he set off for Mother Rose's home.

"Mother Rose, it is morning," he called. "Mother Rose, please wake up."

Mother Rose whispered in a tired voice, "Look, little squirrel. Look at my lowest branch. It took much of my energy, but I coaxed it to be born."

Forrest looked at her lowest branch. There, among the empty briars and thorns, was one single red rose bud. It was the most beautiful rose he had ever seen.

"It is yours, my child," Mother Rose whispered. "Chew off my branch and bring it to your Corinne. Let her know how much you love her."

Forrest chewed the branch neatly and gently, so as not to hurt Mother Rose. He carried it carefully within his little paws and walked to Corinne's tree.

"Happy Valentine's Day, Corinne!" he chattered.

Corinne could scarcely believe her eyes. "Where did you find such a beautiful rose in the dead of winter?" she squeaked.

"A very dear friend gave it to me. She told me to give it to the one I truly love."

Corinne sighed. She leaned toward Forrest's check and gave him a big squirrel kiss. "All I have for you is a basket of seeds and acorns," she whispered.

"That is PERFECT!" Forrest answered. "Just what I wished for!"

Forrest and Corrine spent many, many winters together. They celebrated each and every Valentine's Day under a very special rosebush in the woodlands. Very quietly, so as not to disturb her sleep, they kissed under her branches. Mother Rose always knew. She waited each winter for the loving couple to return.

Your Hand in Mine

In a Northern land of storms by the sea, a cruel king ruled the chieftains and clans of his kingdom. King Bryan loved no one, not even his beautiful daughter. For him, she was a possession like any other, to be traded to the best buyer. And her beauty promised quite a trade for the ambitions of a man without either heart or soul.

Ancient woodlands surrounded his kingdom. But his castle was never grand enough; timber was always needed to build more fortresses and towers.

There were fairies in his kingdom—not under his rule, of course. But they lived in those woodlands and saw too many of the ancient trees being felled each day. Chieftains and clansmen feared the fairy folk. Size had no relevance; a tiny fairy could seize a giant's final breath, and the people of the land all knew it. If truth be told, even the cruel king feared them.

One night, while asleep in his chamber, the king had an unannounced royal visitor. The King of the Fairies had entered through his window and now sought audience with the ruler. Though tiny in size, the Fairy King Stefan was brave and kind. He risked much coming here this way. One swat of the sleeping king's arm could kill him. Nevertheless, he flew up to the king's face and caused the king's nose to twitch, which immediately awakened him.

In a sleepy haze, King Bryan first thought an insect buzzed by. But in the moonlit room, by the fire's hearth, the king's keen eyes saw a very tiny man. Adorned in the richest of clothes, with a golden crown on his head, the Fairy King spoke. "I have come to give a warning and make a request," Stefan said in a stern whisper.

"YOU, little man, give a warning and request of ME?!" The cruel king's voice boomed in the quiet night.

"Perhaps you do not know the fairy strength," the tiny king answered. With that, a heavy chair flew across the bedchamber, breaking in pieces against the door. "Heed my warning, cruel man. Do not destroy our woodlands." With that, the tiny king flew to the window. Before he left, though, he turned to King Bryan and spoke his request. "I wish your beautiful daughter Innes for my bride."

Bryan laughed. Suddenly, the royal bed lifted in the air and landed with a heavy thud on the floor. "Don't deny a fairy request, foolish man! Tell Innes to wait by the lake's edge tomorrow evening at midnight. If she isn't there, I will be here again for you!" With that, King Stefan disappeared in the night.

Suddenly, the King's guards raced into the chamber. "Are you all right?" they asked.

"Leave me!" ordered Bryan. His heart wasn't sorrowful about Innes' fate. In fact, how fortuitous, he thought! Now he wouldn't face a large dowry at the time of her arranged marriage with another powerful chieftain. "Let the fairies have her," he muttered to himself and went back to sleep.

Innes was a gentle girl, with a heart as beautiful as her fair face. She was so unlike her father that those in the castle wondered how such a kind creature could have ever been nurtured under his roof. Innes' mother died when she was two. Nurses and nannies cared for her these past sixteen years. She rarely spoke with her father. Her friends were the servants and workers of the castle, the horses and hounds her father kept as pets and battle companions, and all the creatures of the surrounding woodlands.

At sunrise, King Bryan called for Innes' nurse. The old woman was inconsolable at the news. "Get out, stupid woman," the king roared. "Just make sure she is there, or you won't see tomorrow!!!"

That evening, the nurse dressed Innes in her finest royal gown. She wove flowers in her long, golden braid. "I always dreamed a kind man would take you for his wife. Be safe, my dearest girl," she cried.

"Do not worry, my dear nurse," Innes answered. "I do not fear the woodlands or the fairies. My heart knows I will be safe within their keeping."

Midnight found the beautiful princess by lakeside, moonlight shimmering on her golden tresses. A rustling in the hedge brought a kingdom of tiny fairies to her side. They tossed flower petals, played whistles, and danced among her feet. Innes laughed with a happiness she had never known in the castle.

Then, King Stefan appeared with guards and trumpeters surrounding him. He flew to Innes' hand and alighted within her palm. "I place my hand in yours," he said, gently touching her with his tiny fingers. "I place my heart in your keeping," he whispered.

Innes felt strange, as if she were floating or flying. The world looked different, larger. But it was the same. It was *she* who had changed. She was smaller now, and she could FLY!

Stefan spoke. "Many years ago, a baby was born in your father's castle. The birth of such child was foretold in fairy legends. She was to be a cruel girl filled with magick and darkness. So cruel a child, the sorrow broke her mother's heart, ending her life. We took that child and replaced her with one of our own, a child filled with light and love. We hoped this child could change an evil man, but nothing could shift such cruelty. Now, we take you back, fair Innes. You will be my Fairy Queen and rule these woodlands with love and kindness."

Innes looked into Stefan's handsome face. "I place my hand in yours," she whispered. "I place my heart in your keeping."

As for the cruel king, neighboring chieftains overtook his throne, hoping to kidnap his beautiful daughter, Innes. But no one ever saw her again.

www.ingramcontent.com/pod-product-compliance
Lightning Source LLC
Chambersburg PA
CBHW030558130626
46552CB00006B/2591